SUPERHEROES CLUB

By Madeleine Sherak, PhD

Illustrated by Esther Yee Sol Choi

MY BENCH PRODUCTIONS

In memory of Tommy, my husband of 46 years, who will always inspire me to live life according to the values we embraced as husband and wife, as parents and as grandparents.

I dedicate this book to our three children, Barbra, Melissa and William and to their children - our ten grandchildren.

Tommy lived his life helping to make the world a better place and teaching them to do the same. I hope that my books will inspire other children to embrace those same values.

Publisher's Cataloging-in-Publication

Sherak, Madeleine, 1949- author.
Superheroes Club / by Madeleine Sherak ; illustrator, Esther YeeSol Choi.
pages cm -- (Superheroes Club)
SUMMARY: Lily is a second-grader who rallies her friends at school to form a club dedicated to helping their community--a superheroes club.
Audience: Ages 5-8.
ISBN 9780997785807

1. Heroes--Juvenile fiction. 2. Clubs--Juvenile fiction. 3. Voluntarism--Juvenile fiction. 4. Helping behavior--Juvenile fiction. [1. Heroes--Fiction. 2. Clubs--Fiction. 3. Voluntarism--Fiction. 4. Helpfulness--Fiction.] I. Choi, Esther Yee Sol, illustrator. II. Title. III. Series: Sherak, Madeleine, 1949- Superheroes Club (Series)

PZ7.1.S5155Su 2017   [E]
QBI16-900052

Edited by Cheri Dellelo

For information regarding permission write to
My Bench Productions
26500 Agoura Road Suite 102-751,
Calabasas, CA 91302.

Published by My Bench Productions 2017

Distributed by Greenleaf Book Group

For ordering information or special discounts for bulk purchases, please contact Greenleaf Book Group at PO Box 91869, Austin, TX 78709, 512.891.6100.

Manufactured by Asia Pacific Offset on acid-free paper
Manufactured in Guang Dong, China on June 26, 2017
Batch No. Q17040208-R02

It was the first week back at school after summer vacation and Lily woke up with a SMile.

Lily skipped to her closet, singing, "I AM ME, I LIKE ME, THAT'S WHO I AM!"

She tugged a little too hard at a dress hanging up,

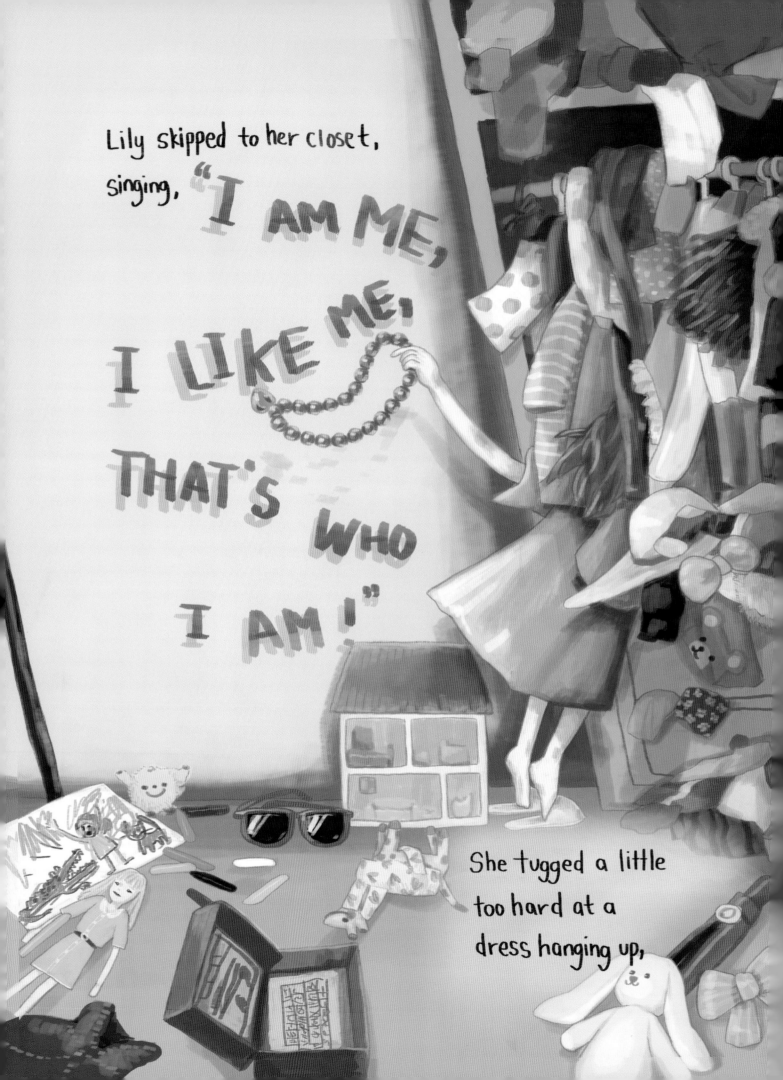

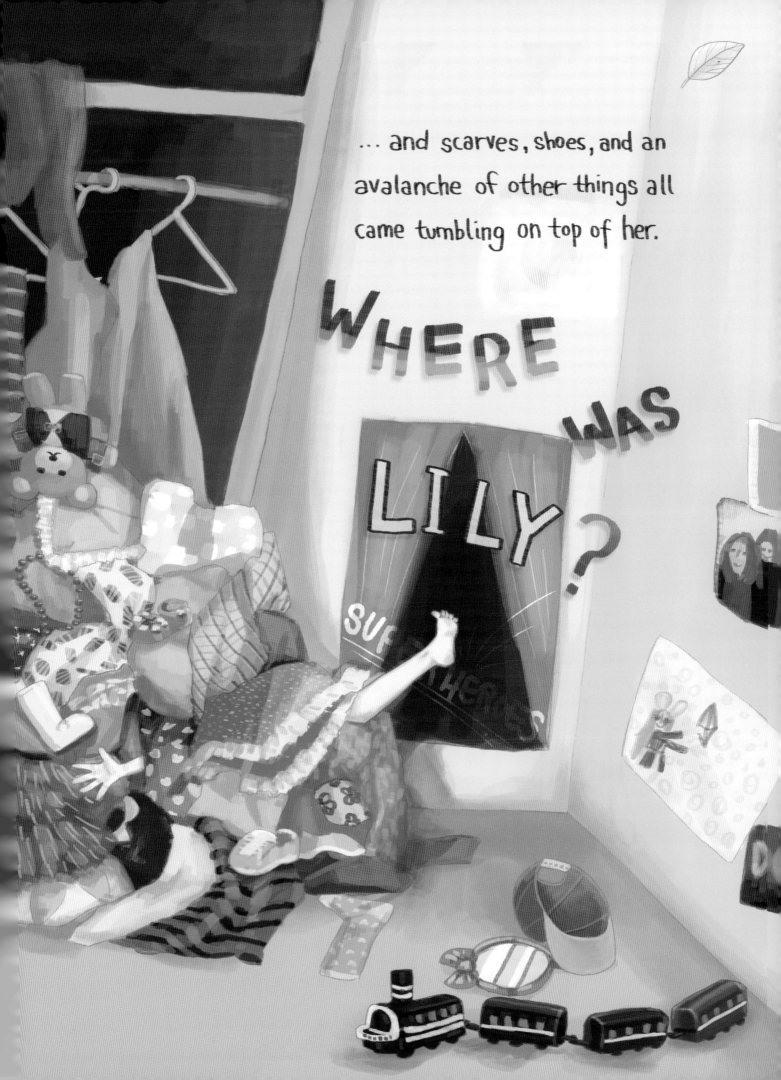

Suddenly, Lily popped out from under the enormous mountain of clothes...
fully dressed!

"**Your** outfit is colorful today!" said her mom when Lily came downstairs for breakfast.

Lily twirled around and sang,

"I AM ME, I LIKE ME, THAT'S WHO I AM!"

"I LIKE you too," said her mom, smiling.

Anxious to get to school, Lily was gulping down her cereal when her mom asked,

"Have you thought about what you'll bring to school for Share Day? Remember, it has to be something related to what you did over summer vacation."

Lily looked up from her bowl and all around the kitchen as she thought. Then, her gaze stopped on a sign that had always hung above the kitchen sink.

SHARING & CARING

Her eyes lit up...
She had a **GREAT IDEA!**

Lily got to Wilbarmel Elementary School just as Mr. Thomas was opening the door to his classroom.

When everyone was seated, Mr. Thomas called on Alex to share what he had done during his summer vacation.

Alex introduced MEATBALL🐾, the new service dog his family had adopted over the summer. Alex has autism spectrum disorder, and he told the class how Meatball helps him from being uncomfortable in crowds and new situations, just like Miss Angela helps him in the classroom.

Joaquin stood up next.
"I played **roller hockey**," he announced.
He then did *wheelies* around the class
in his athletic shoes, showing everyone his
WINNING hockey moves.

Many of the children cheered, saying things like, "WAY TO GO, JOAQUIN!" Even Mr. Thomas chimed in with "SCORE!!!" Joaquin gave everyone high-fives.

Then, it was Mia's turn.
With Mr.Thomas's help, she projected a video on
the white board showing her doing a series of flips.

"I went to the State Gymnastics Championships,"
Mia proudly told the class.

"And I can finally do a split leap on the balance beam!"

Everyone cheered for Mia, too.

Finally, Lily stood up. "I'm a SUPERHERO.
I'm a SHARING, CARING SUPERHERO!" she announced.
"How could she be a superhero?" the children's faces seemed to ask.
She didn't **look** like a superhero. Lily knew what they were thinking.
"It's not how you **look** that makes you a superhero, but what you DO,"
Lily explained confidently.

Lily then explained how, during the summer, she had collected jackets, hats, gloves, shoes, toys, sports equipment, books and games for the community relief drive at the fire station.

"I'm going to see Fireman Mike this afternoon," Lily told the class.
"You can come to my house after school and see what I collected."

"Great idea!" said Mr. Thomas.

After school, Lily and her dad were busy organizing her closet when the doorbell rang.

When Lily's mom opened the front door, there stood Alex, Miss Angela, Joaquin, and Mia with their arms filled with things. Meatball was there too, and even he was carrying a bucket in his mouth!

"Lily told us to come and see what she collected for Fireman Mike. We thought we'd bring some of our own things too," said Mia.

The children rushed upstairs and dumped everything on
Lily's floor.
"Now, we can ALL be superheroes," said Lily.

"Nah, if you don't have SUPER powers, you can't be a SUPERHERO,"
said Joaquin.

Lily explained, "If you believe in yourself, you can help other kids too."

"OK, but what else can we do besides helping Fireman Mike?" asked Alex.

"Just like Meatball helps you, we can help other kids, just in other ways," said Lily.

"Some kids get bullied at school.

Some kids are sad because they eat lunch alone,

and some kids never get picked to play sports."

"OK, OK, I get it. We could definitely help those kids," said Joaquin, already thinking about ways he might help.

"Yeah, let's join forces and call ourselves the SUPERHEROES CLUB," suggested Mia.

"Yes! and sharing and caring is what we'll do," added Lily.

Lily gave each member of
the new Superheroes Club,
including Meatball,
a "Superhero" power band.
She explained, "Whenever
we wear these power bands
to school, everyone will know
who we are and what we do."

"I think I can get into this Superhero stuff," said Joaquin. "Me too," said Mia and Alex in unison. And even Meatball barked in agreement.

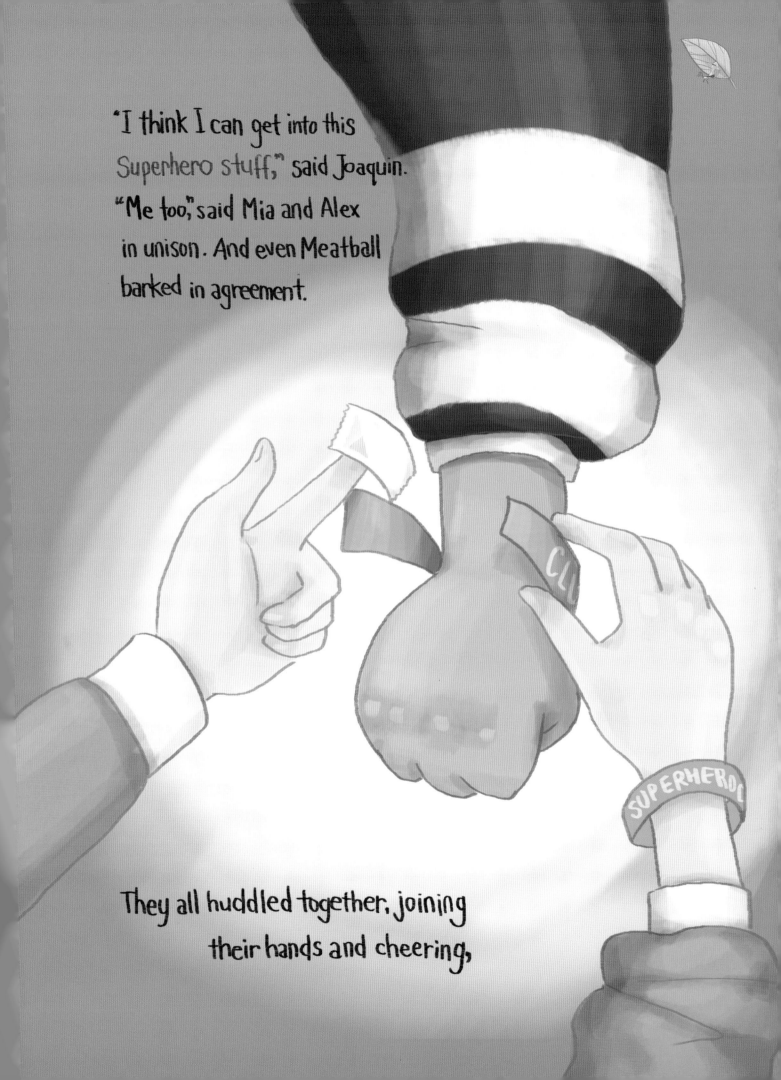

They all huddled together, joining their hands and cheering,

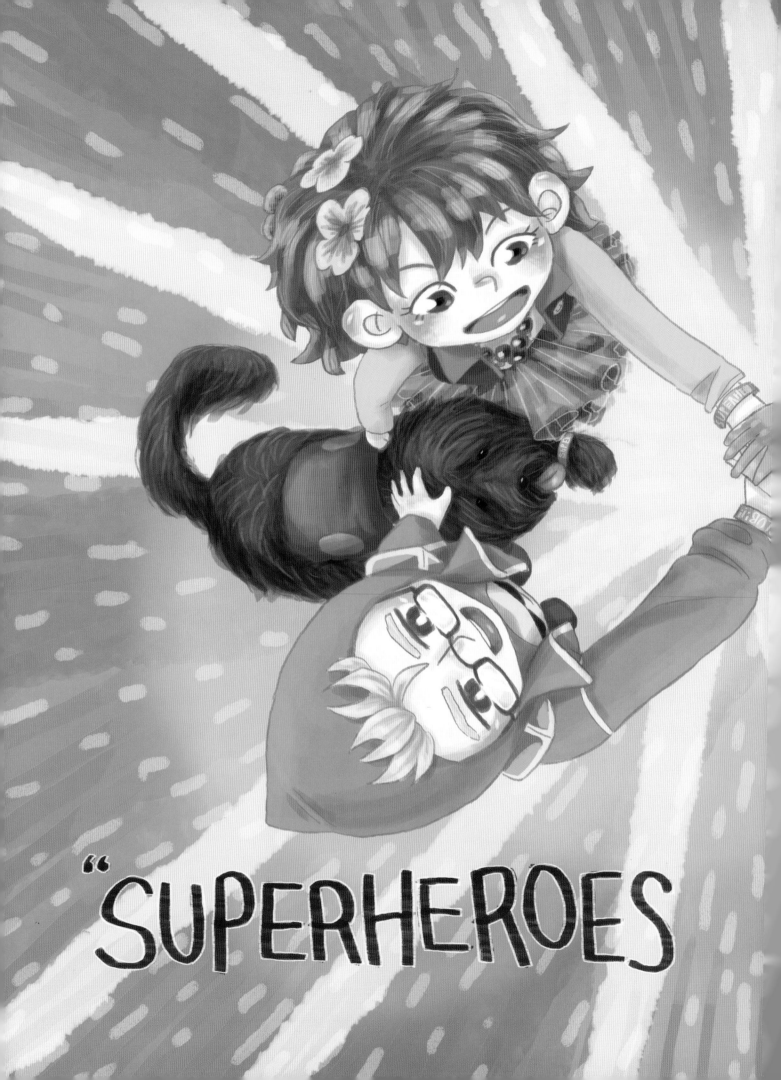

"SUPERHEROES

"Superheroes have special missions. So, what's ours?" asked Joaquin.

"There's a carnival at the fire station today and we're going there first," said Lily.

The superheroes gathered the things on Lily's floor, piled them into a wagon, and marched to the fire station with Miss Angela and Lily's mother and father.

Meatball tagged along, picking up falling items all along the way.

When they got to the station, Lily introduced all the superheroes to Fireman Mike.

"We're here to help kids!" she announced. "And here are all the things we collected."

"GREAT JOB!" said Fireman Mike. "Our carnival is just beginning."

The superheroes dropped all the things they had collected in the big bins near the dunk tank. To their surprise, Mr. Thomas was also helping at the carnival-he was in the dunk tank!

The superheroes all agreed- Mr. Thomas was good at helping kids. So, they made him a member of their Superheroes Club too and gave him a POWER band.

...right before dunking him!

If you were a superhero, how would you help people?